THE
ADVENTURES
of a
B OK'S
LIFE

THE ADVENTURES

of a

B**OO**K'S

LIFE

MARY E. HAYNES

iUniverse

THE ADVENTURES OF A BOOK'S LIFE

iUniverse books may be ordered through booksellers or by contacting:

iUniverse
1663 Liberty Drive
Bloomington, IN 47403
www.iuniverse.com
844-349-9409

Because of the dynamic nature of the Internet, any web addresses or links contained in this book may have changed since publication and may no longer be valid. The views expressed in this work are solely those of the author and do not necessarily reflect the views of the publisher, and the publisher hereby disclaims any responsibility for them.

Any people depicted in stock imagery provided by Getty Images are models, and such images are being used for illustrative purposes only. Certain stock imagery © Getty Images.

ISBN: 978-1-5320-9837-6 (sc)
ISBN: 978-1-5320-9838-3 (e)

Print information available on the last page.

iUniverse rev. date: 01/22/2021

To Jason Thompson,

I hope you enjoy my efforts.

Mary E. Hayner

I am also very thankful to Linda Witvoet for her inspiration for my books' illustrations.

CHAPTER 1

WHO AM I?

Who am I? I would like to introduce myself, I am a book and I talk to myself, I talk to myself a lot. It might be said that, that makes me crazy, but I'm not crazy. How do I know I'm not crazy? First of all, I make a lot of sense to myself and second no one has carried me off to the loony bin... yet. So, I'm not crazy.

Now, as to why I talk to myself so much. There is nothing to talk to where I'm at! That is, if I really talk, maybe I just think I talk because I have so many ideas. And I can hear. I hear myself and others also. Okay, okay, my gosh! Hearing voices too, you really must think I've gone off the deep end! Whether I talk to myself or I'm just thinking, really doesn't matter, so let's just call it communicating. After all, I'm just a book. As to the other reason I communicate with myself. It's because it gets pretty dark and depressing until by chance I get opened up and read, I just love that. I love hearing other books being read out loud too.

About my age, I really don't know it. The page of my birth is never open long enough for me to get a good feel for it. Of course, I don't remember being born or being created for that matter. I don't remember a family either. I just know that I'm here. I don't feel old nor do I feel young. I don't like the term "middle-aged", so let's just say I'm a little mature. I have a nice amber colored cover and lovely pages, a little worn and frayed around the edges, but still lovely and I have a nice straight spine.

I am almost as wide as I am tall which, is a good feature in a book, and my pages don't number a lot, which is also a plus to lots of readers. I do have a few wrinkles on my cover and a few faded spots which I dislike, but that comes from a little maturity, doesn't it? Oh, by the way, I have heard, well heard, when my pages are open that, "I'm a good read", I think that's a nice compliment, don't you?

I am also psychic. I know, I know what you're going to say, there is no such thing, but I really am. I can "Judge a book by its cover". I get feelings from other books all the time. For example, I was placed by a book called "The Wizard of Oz." That was a very unsettling experience. My spine tingled all the time and the flying monkeys were quite unsettling not to mention the witch and the wizard.

At this time I think you should know more about books in general and who we are and who I am, I get the feeling that almost all of the other books feel like I do.

First of all, you have to realize that all of us have feelings. We can feel pain, we can get emotional, we can smell, we can see (I think I need glasses!) and we can hear. That is, if we listen real hard. I don't think that we feel pain or are as emotional as readers are. I don't know how this is possible but that's just the way it is. I am one of the few books that I know that have mastered the art of listening and I try hard not to get my feelings hurt.

These are some of the things we absolutely detest. Being placed down opened face with our spines jutting into the air. It is very uncomfortable and frankly a little painful. While we're on the subject of pain, might I mention the thing called "dog earring", whoever invented that should have their ears "dog eared" too, OUCH!!

I think that the most devastating thing that we have had to endure is having greasy food eaten while we are being read. Talk about gross and adding years to ones age! Drops of grease are left on our pages, only to be smeared and smeared until the spot is no longer just a spot. It has a life of its own. It just grows and grows and grows. It permeates itself to page after page of muck. It will never come out, it will never leave and dirt affixes itself so quickly it's unbelievable. It's very difficult to read the words, it's very unattractive and we all detest it.

Also being thrown around and having our pages torn or even worse ripped out, not only are we not whole anymore, but, bruised from the inside and out.

The last thing I will mention is, not the big of a deal, but it is bothersome. When our pages are just being thumbed though time and time again, not a word read, just thumbing though, it's quite dizzying and makes us feel like spinning tops.

Now on a more positive note, the things we love about being books are, of course, being read. We and especially me, love, love, love our margins being written on, it's just a wonderful feeling. The side of the readers palm on, our leafs, the caress of the pen strokes on our pages and in our margins, the fact that the reader left a little of itself for other readers.... well, it is comforting and I like it.

We also like to be touched, well, most of us do. I think that being touched is as close to being hugged as any book can get, that is except for by the younger readers. They do hug, not really hug, almost "strangle", is the word. They don't mean any harm, actually it is kind of endearing but it is hard to get any air or concentrate on anything else.

Being smelled is very nice, it doesn't happen that often but when it's done we get a feeling of satisfaction that we've really done our jobs. By the way, I have to brag. I have been smelled more often than most of the books I know, well, at least up till now. I have always wanted to be one of those big leather bound books, that smell just wonderful but I'm not, I'm just a small plain book.

I don't know about the other books but one of my most favorite things is when a reader reads me over and over. Being taken off the shelf and being reread, knowing that the reader is getting a little something different from me with each reading is extremely pleasurable just knowing that I'm not dull or stale or unwanted is wonderful.

One thing I haven't been able to grasp, not yet that is. I have felt from other books that some of their fondest memories have been in a home and the reader snuggles up in a blanket and reads them by the side of a fire. Usually the reader sips from a glass that has liquid with an amber tint to it. My cover is amber. Maybe that will happen to me, at least my color and the glass would match.

CHAPTER 2

WHERE HAVE I BEEN?

I have been to lots of places, (I think that can account for my maturity too). One of the first places I can remember being at is a library. It wasn't exactly the biggest library in the world and I was kind of glad of that. A library is supposed to be quiet but it wasn't, at least not for me. It took me a long time to get use to all the noise and to me being shuffled around, (the readers never put me back on my prober shelf). I was always being put in a different place, like next to books I could barely stand, for instance the Dictionary. I know that the Dictionary is a necessary evil and has its purpose, but really, it is so full of itself and thinks it knows everything, it just drones on and on all day about how all the readers need it. I have heard that encyclopedias' are worse. Can you even imagine?

And getting use to all the reading out loud and the books trying to communicate at the same time in the library almost drove me nuts. It was extremely hard to concentrate on the contents of just one book. I wanted so much to know it all.

And then, I was put near the children's section, what a pleasant surprise. I say pleasant because in my experience the younger the reader the more roughly I was treated, but not here. Almost all day long one story after another was being read out loud, talk about enjoying my stay on the shelf. At night I would imagine that I was in the story of the sleeping princess or in a story of the hero saving the day.

I did feel a little guilty though. Because it didn't bother me not being picked up and read, touched, enjoyed and admired. Which as you know is a books true purpose and goal.

I was just getting adjusted to the library when I found myself in a "used book" store, why a "used book", store, I asked myself. ("Used book." Sounds like the book is all used up, am I all used up? NOT). I never figured out the answer. Nor do I know how I got here. I must have dozed off. I was very glad that I had come from a library to a small place because I had already gotten use to all the commotion at a bigger place and going smaller was a very easy adjustment. Can you imagine going from a small place to a big one? It would be overwhelming!

The "used book" store was fun, I was always placed in a different area, "A Book about Town", you might say, I heard and felt a lot of different books there. I remember a book about exercise. I can't quite remember its name, as far as I am concerned they pretty much all have the same message and this one advertised it every day. This exercise is for the abs, this exercise is for the thighs, this exercise if for the pecks. By the way, what are pecks? Maybe I should ask Dictionary? Nah, I think I'll pass.

Then, out of the blue, all the books were being moved or I should say thrown in bins, (one of my pet peeves, being thrown around.)

I had always thought that a "used book" store had much more respect for books. It wasn't until later that I realized, we were, being tossed around by movers. We were being moved! Where were we going? How exciting!

That's when the other book dropped. A huge book was thrown in the bin I was in, right atop of me, ugh! I couldn't move nor could I get I off me. I really should have paid more attention to the exercise book.

I kept trying to get a feel for this monster, but I got nothing, I mean NOTHING! At that moment a strange thought struck me. Is it possible that a book this big might not have anything to communicate? How would that be possible? Does this book have any words or any ideas in it?

A book this big had to, didn't it? That is the way it seemed to me, it had to have something in it... something. I haven't been by or near a book that hasn't communicated something to me. So this was very strange. Where is a philosophy book when you need one?

Since there was no way that I was going to find a self help book in the mess we were all in, with every book complaining and moaning about being squished, I decided to try and relax and get through this horrible ordeal. After a while our bin began to move. Where are we going? Wow, it looked like we were going outside and I like the outdoors. What a shock! Outside was extremely cold. I have never felt that cold, EVER.

I've felt it slightly from other books but never had I experienced anything like it myself.

As we approached the icy cold outdoors, I started to feel very grateful that the monster was atop of me. It was actually keeping me warm with its mass! My leafs stopped fluttering and all of the dampness was being sucked up by this monster. Was that the purpose of this book? To protect the rest of us in a time of need? I wondered.

We were outside until it was almost dark. I was starting to worry about being put into the trash bin. All of a sudden we were on the move again, back inside the "used book" store. What had happened? As soon as we entered, I knew what had happened, a new paint job for "used book" store.

What a relief, but the smell of the paint was awful, another thing I would have to endure, but, at least, we were back inside where it was warm and feels safe. Not only did the "used book" store get a new paint job but, carpets and shelves had been refinished. For a while I was totally disoriented. All the sections had been rearranged and placed in different areas. It was going to take some time getting use to all the new arrangements and where was I going to be placed? Please, please not behind the register, not one book gets read from there.

Thankfully, I wasn't placed there. I was pretty much left by myself for a nice piece of time, which I enjoyed. I could think about myself and all that I had been though up till now. It was odd spending time alone. But, I enjoyed it. I wouldn't want to be alone all the time, but there is something relaxing about it. Let my leafs down, so to speak. The solitude didn't last long. I hope it happens again, not for long periods just once in awhile. I can see where it would get lonely but every so often it's nice.

Next, I found myself in the "Romantic Novel" section. That was very interesting. All of these readers seeking love or romantic relationships, I found it all a bit bewildering but they did get to go to all kinds of fun places. I also found out something about myself that was very special to me. I found out that for a nice portion of my existence I've been loved, really and truly, how cool is that?

I don't know how long I was in the "used book" store, but it seemed like a long time. And then, a reader bought me, I think I was going to be a gift for a reader, (my pages weren't open long enough for me to figure it out). I was placed in a bag, Yuk! I was very excited though, not only about "maybe" being a gift but finally, I hoped, I was going to a residence, a family of readers. Where I could take my time and get to know all the other books in the shared space, not to be shuffled around all the time, to actually have a real home. Boy was I wrong!

It was a DUMP, a real dump, so you can imagine how mistreated I was. I was rarely taken down from the shelf, except when I was used as a "door stop". That was extremely unpleasant! I was never read. The place reeked! It smelt like old garbage and I was even used as a "stepping stone"! Me, a "stepping stone"! The only saving grace about being there was "no grease spots!"

And then there was a fire, a FIRE! I only escaped the flames with my binding in tack because of the firemen who put out the fire before I was too damaged. I really must tell you. There are three things that books are afraid of they are FIRE, WATER and the TRASH BIN.

I was so relieved when the firemen showed up, that the water was not much of a concern. I was lucky I hadn't been drenched. I would have been thrown in the trash bin in a flash. I was slightly wet and my pages fringed somewhat. Some of my pages stuck together, it took time to get them unstuck.

I got a dank smell too. Which has lasted longer than I had hoped. It still lingers a bit.

That doesn't mean I'm older than I am. I know you think I'm a little obsessed with age, well, wouldn't you be if you didn't know how old you were? I even caught a cold. I creaked and my spine ached. I felt damp and couldn't get warm until I was taken outside and placed in the sun.

I love being outside. Most of the time that I have been taken out doors is a real treat. My pages are open. The warmth of the sun on my pages and spine, now that is very relaxing. My pages are even turned slower. I feel more cherished and wanted when I'm in the rays of the sun.

My happiness was short lived though. Yes, you guessed it, back to the "used book" store. I did have some interesting times there. I'll just make the best of it until hopefully I find a real home or at least my idea of a real home.

One thing about the "used book" store is, it doesn't seem to change much, so I fit back in very quickly. That is, I fit in until a reader placed me by a book with beautiful pictures of landscapes. It had an exquisite cover. I couldn't get a good feel for the book, maybe that's because it was mostly pictures and I've never got a good feel for picture books. I felt completely out of place, I kept trying to look my best but to no avail.

All the other books in this area paid no attention to me at all. They kept up a clamor all the time, "Wow look at that book". "Isn't it beautiful". And worst of all, "the book" was constantly being picked up, looked at, fondled and read, well, read is a big stretch of the imagination, since it hardly had any words! Yes, I was a tad envious and I know it was mean to get pleasure from the readers who picked up the exquisite book and just thumbed through it. But I did! The thumbing of the pages seemed to happen often, or at least often enough for me.

So, there I was being basically miserable on the shelf when I remembered something. Why hadn't I thought of this before? Could it really work? It had happened at the library. A reader had placed me next to book on "Positive Thinking". (Yes, I know what you're going to say). I believe in being psychic, but not, positive thinking.

Well, I could at least give it a try, so I did. I tried to remember all about the meditating and chanting before I started. So I began, over and over ad over, "move me off this shelf, move me off this shelf move me off this shelf! Project, project, I told myself. I was only successful in putting myself into a trance. For how long, who knows?

All of a sudden, I was jerked awake when a reader grabbed me and shoved me open faced into its' pocket. I can tell you I was plenty scared. It was so dark in its' pocket and it smelled odd too. I was trying to get my bearings when I heard bells go off and heard readers running and yelling all around me. I was then quickly and violently dropped to the floor along with a number of other books.

After all the excitement had died away, I was placed on a shelf at the front of the "used book" store, which by the way, is one of the best spots to be placed in, at any store. I was checking out the other books that were occupying this wonderful space, when I felt them, ALL of THEM. "A reader tried to steal you". "Are you all right?" "Are you damaged in any way?" "You must be important if a reader wanted to steal you." I was really taken aback, shocked and dumbfounded! It was rather wonderful to be the center of attention and I relished it. I tried to keep the fact that two of my pages had been torn in the scuffle to myself, why spoil all of the attention?

Then a revelation came to me, I completely understood the book with the exquisite cover. To be fondled and babied all the time was very, very nice. It wasn't the books fault. I knew deep within me that, those special treatments won't last the lifetime of a book. It will, eventually fade. So, "enjoy it while you can," I did.

At that same time I had another revelation. If ever I had the opportunity to try and use "Positive Thinking" again, I will be more explicit in my meditations and chants. For example: "Move me off this shelf and move me to another shelf within the store," "move me off this shelf and move me to another shelf within the store."

While I was at the front of the "used book" store I had an extremely rewarding experience. I have never been placed next to a real adventure book before. Fantasies, yes, but never a real adventure story. Never. And how well it communicated with me! It made me feel like I was part of its' adventure. It was called, "The Adventures of Tom Sawyer".

It was exhilarating, exciting, fun, lots of mischief and intrigue. The story had everything in it that I would imagine an adventure story should have. I especially enjoyed the rides on the raft traveling along the banks of the Mississippi River. Just lazily floating down the river, no rushing around, no place in particular to go, just to drift and dream. I know that I'm not that fond of water, but it felt so peaceful. And, it is just imagination after all.

There was even a story about a fairy. She could fly! Can you imagine, being able to fly? To soar in the sky and go any where you want to go, to perch on the highest mountain and see the world in all its' beauty. Wow. I would love it!

I spent so much time as a part of the "Tom Sawyer" and the fairy book that I didn't even realize that I had been brought up to the cash register! I was being bought! Again!

Quick, quick, "positive thinking," I didn't even have time to form any kind of meditation plan or chant, I just started, "not a dump", "not a dump", "not a dump"!

CHAPTER 3

WHERE AM I GOING?

The reader that bought me seemed pleasant. It had a nice smell and it was taking me outside, yep outside. I wasn't cold at all, the sun was shining and it felt warm on my cover and spine. I wasn't put in a bag this time, maybe that was a good sign. I sure hoped so. The reader got into a motor vehicle and placed me on a cushion. (You noticed, not thrown me, placed, yes, this was a very good beginning).

I was somewhat apprehensive. I can only remember being in a motor vehicle three other times and one of those times was to the "DUMP". At this moment I really tried to give myself a pep talk to forget about the "DUMP" and concentrate on this new beginning.

I started to relax when the reader opened the windows of the vehicle and the fresh air flowed in and made my pages flicker in the breeze. I could hear soft music playing. This was different, but very agreeable. The vehicle stopped and I was taken for a walk, wow, a, walk outside. Into a shop I went, I couldn't tell where I was, but I did notice a pamphlet called, coffee prices. Next, my cover was opened and I was being read. The aroma was engulfing. I was in a dreamy state when I realized that my cover had been opened and I didn't catch a feel for my age before the page was turned. Darn!

I began to believe that this adventure wasn't going to be so bad after all. Was I going to be staying with this reader in a home?

I was in a daze, so I don't know how I came to be outside. But there I was being read again, I was at pool,

I could smell the chlorine and enjoyed it immensely. Maybe, I was a dolphin in a "past life". Oh get over it, a "past life"! I have a hard enough time with this one. The reader closed my cover and placed me under a towel, I guess to keep me out of the sun or to keep me from getting wet. Wasn't that thoughtful!

I knew then that this reader was serious about keeping me. Treating me the way any book should be treated or would want to be treated. I was overjoyed. I wished I could have expressed to this reader how I felt but I couldn't. I decided then and there to always be on my best behavior and never give cause for this reader to get rid of me. Even if I was to be placed near or by Dictionary! I will not complain, I won't cause any trouble. Oh, I hope this reader doesn't notice my two torn pages! Will that make a difference on how this reader treats me? Stop this right now! It's just going to ruin my moment of bliss. Focus on only the good yes, yes, I will and I did.

I was exhausted after being on such an emotional roller coaster. When I was back in the vehicle, I just let myself drift, not doing much of anything except enjoying being on a cushion with a breeze flowing over me and sun on my cover.

The vehicle was stopped and I was taken into the readers, HOME! As soon as I was walked in, I felt all cozy and comfortable. What a wonderful feeling. The reader put me on a counter, I was bewildered, why a counter? I shortly found out. The reader opened me up and placed another book in the middle of me, what's happening? This isn't what I expected. Oh NO, the reader had opened me up to my torn pages. I've been found out!

Then, the most amazing thing happened. I could feel the rips of my pages being mended. It felt so soothing. I was almost whole again. I knew it. I had found a home! I never doubted it, well almost never doubted. My wonderful new reader cared about me! My reader left me on the counter, I guess so my pages wouldn't stick together after being mended. I was being healed. Did you notice, "That reader or this reader is now MY READER, It was nice to be left on the on the counter.

It gave me a chance to get a feel for my home and to let it sink in that a reader was mine.

I don't think I have ever been in a kitchen before. I knew it was a kitchen because of the cookbook I was placed next to once. The cookbook had been right. The "Kitchen" is the heart of the house. I could feel it. I decided to take my time and soak it all in and enjoy my new found home. I could detect a big room off the kitchen where there were books. Books!

This was going to be a pleasure. I love getting to know other books I've never met before. I did have one dreaded thought. Dictionary will probably be here, somewhere.

After I was healed and put on an oak bookcase, I've never smelled oak before, nice. Anyway, I soon found out that Dictionary was never around that much. It seemed that only one book at a time had to put with all of it's bragging. Interesting... I did meet lots of new books and I was shocked to find a number of books that I already knew there. I know I will love it here, my new home.

I was read so much. I even got to be in bed. How special is that. The atmosphere of my new digs was engrossing. I was taken to different rooms and in almost every room there were books. I never knew that homes were made up of so many rooms with books everywhere. One place I wasn't particularly fond of was the bathroom. Thankfully, I wasn't taken in there often.

One day when I was just lingering with my thoughts. I was taken from my shelf and placed on the counter, much to my surprise, I wasn't nervous in the least. My pages were opened and written on again, nice, very nice. I could tell from my reader that something special was about to happen. There was food being packed up and I'm not sure, but I think a bottle of soda was there too. I was put into a bag with all the other stuff, I must admit I worried about being so close to the food but I wasn't worried about the bag thing, how refreshing.

Out to the vehicle I went. Actually I was excited. I didn't think too much about where I was being taken, I knew that this was going to be an adventure. Maybe, a little like "Tom Sawyer?" I hoped so.

I ended up at another readers' home, not exactly an adventure I told myself.

The confusion and the noise drowned out most of my thoughts. I was taken out of the bag along with the food and the bottle of wine and placed on a table. Six other books were on the table with me, but I was just far enough away that I couldn't get a read on them.

All six readers sat down at the table and started talking. The food was everywhere. Was I going to read while my reader ate greasy food? No, no, no, this can't be happening! Whew, my reader didn't eat while reading me. (Thank you. Thank you.) That's when I noticed all the other books. They were all me! Not exactly me. One was years older than me. Another one was much younger and one had tons of grease spots on it and in it! The older book was being read, it had all of my words but the words just flowed gracefully and gave new meaning to the words that I had inside of me. Then the younger one was read, and all my words sounded full of giggles. Next the "grease spot" was read but I could hardly understand a word of what was being read. All of these books had my words in them. How is that possible?

The answer was soon to follow. I'm at a book club! Me, myself and I, had been chosen for a book club meeting. Spectacular, marvelous! I had no idea that there were so many of me. I had a family! I was a family of sextuplets. We were all different to be sure, yet all of them were, me. Immediately I started doing my best to communicate with my family! It was very difficult with all the reading out loud and the din of the conversation I did manage to get a bit of information. Most of them had no idea where they came from either. They had feelings and emotions. They could hear and communicate. The only one that could communicate better than me was the older version of me. It told me that a books life was too short to worry about such things as "where we come from", or "why we have feelings and emotions or "why or how" we can communicate. Just "try and relax and enjoy the ride". Before I knew it the club meeting was over. I was disappointed to be taken away so soon after getting acquainted with my family, but I couldn't help but wonder. If there are six books like me, might there be others?

"I can't think about that now, I'll think about that tomorrow." I've heard that before, somewhere...

Aaah... Home at last. I was placed in my very special place feeling completely tranquil. I didn't feel the need to try and analyze everything I'd been through. I knew that I had been on an adventure. Not like the "Adventure of Tom Sawyer." And certainly not the kind of adventure I expected, but an adventure just the same.

Home had a new meaning for me now, I wasn't alone in this delightful world of books and I had my very own special reader. I was feeling very good about myself when something slid in beside me. I couldn't make out what it was.

It wasn't a book, what was it? Excuse me. I felt the thing beside me communicate, who are you. I am a book and who are you? I live here. You are just "A Blank Page". It replied, "Am not!" and then it started, "Are too!" "Am not!" It responded, "Yeah, well you're just a type-o. Again, "Am not," "Are too!" Stop it I communicated as forcefully as I could and it stopped. (Another thought occurred to me, if I'm read too many times, will I disappear or even worse become a blank page?)

It took a few minutes for me to gather all my ruffled pages to communicate with it again. I began again, "I must apologize, I think we got off on the wrong page, would you care to start over?" "Blank Page" never really actually apologized but we did start to communicate. I found out heaps of information, I don't know how with it being a "Blank Page" nonetheless I did. It seems "Blank Page" has a special relationship with MY READER.

When "Blank Page" gets taken off the shelf, it gets written in and on, WRITTEN. I thought to myself that "Blank Page" must be a Diary. I didn't let "Blank Page" know that, I didn't want to start another argument. We had fantastic communications on the subject of being written on. (Every time I hear it, "written," I get goose bumps. You know how I feel about that). I'll just call "Blank Page" B.P. from now on, I hope B.P. doesn't mind after all I think we're friends.

I was jealous. B.P. was taken off the shelf more than the lot of us put together. The only nice thing about that was when B.P. was returned, B.P. had more feelings, emotions and information to share with all of us. We all felt that we were part of a mystery novel. What's going to happen next?

B.P. returned one night. All I wanted to know, was, what the book was that I felt laying beside B.P. on the table. B.P. didn't know, something called, "How and where to get Published." I wondered what that meant, published. I knew I wouldn't ask Dictionary.

I had a plan. Hopefully B.P. would cooperate. The next rime B.P. was off the shelf, could B.P. please find out from Thesaurus what published meant?

Thesaurus had been placed near the new book and it wouldn't be difficult to gather the information. Thesaurus didn't have the ego that Dictionary has. I was surprised when B.P. agreed. B.P. was gone for longer than I would have wished but when B.P. was finally place back on our shelf, B.P. had the information about being published. I swear B.P. sounded like Dictionary. I almost gagged.

: To be published is: to prepare and produce material in printed or electronic form for distribution and, usually for sale." That's wonderful I interrupted, if I could have hugged B.P. I would have.

All I wanted was to be alone and digest this information. I gently sent out feelings to all the books on our shelf to try and keep their communications down to a minimum. They grudgingly obliged. Books are hardly ever quiet. I don't think most of them need time to themselves like I do.

What does that mean, to prepare and produce material in printed...for distribution...

Oh, Oh, Oh. I've been published! We all have been published. Incredible! I could only think of myself. I've been published! No wonder there are so many of me around, I'm in distribution! I'm probably everywhere.

Then I noticed something I never noticed before, the word, "Author". I repeated it very quietly to myself, "author". A strange feeling overwhelmed me.

CHAPTER 4

THE AWAKENING

I begged and begged B.P., please, the next time you are by Thesaurus you have to find out exactly what "Author" means. B.P. professed to know the meaning. I was indignant. No, I need to know the exact meaning, please don't tell me what you think. I want a real definition. I was on a rampage, all the books on my shelf were threatened with fire, water or going into the trash bin if anyone of them had the information and didn't let me know. I don't think anyone of the books would have told me, even if they had the answer. They were too scared I might follow through with my threats.

I could hardly wait for B.P. to be taken from the shelf. All that mattered was to get close to Thesaurus again. I was so nervous. I wished I could pace. I had a fleeting thought about using "positive thinking" again, but all I could think of was the word "author". I had a feeling I knew what it meant, but I had to be sure, I had to be!

It finally happened. B.P. was taken and placed near Thesaurus. I could barely contain myself. Why didn't B.P. come back? What was taking so long? On and on this went. I knew I was driving the other books crazy but I didn't care. I needed to know and I needed to know now. I've always thought I had been a patient book, I was wrong.

When B.P. returned I communicated, "You took your time." "Did you do it on purpose?" (How could I have been so unthinking, I wasn't going to get any information by attacking B.P.).

B.P. started to profess, "That I really wasn't a friend," "I was just using our friendship to get what I wanted, on and on. I let B.P. rant and finally I interrupted and gave the nicest compliment I could think of, It's just that you have so much savvy and smarts, I know no other book could have done it better."

I could tell B.P. was delighted with that. The response I had been anxiously waiting for finally came: and author is,

1. Writer: somebody who writes a book or other text such as a literary work or report
2. Professional writer: somebody who writes books as a profession
3. Creator or source: the creator or cause of something

I listened very intently. I had been right! I kept thinking that it just might be possible but I didn't dare to hope, there it was, it was true!

I was overwhelmed with joy. I had been written when I was born. I'm not a type-o! An author had written me.

Wave after wave of knowledge was swimming into me. That's why I love the feel of being written on and in, that's why, I have feelings and emotions, that's why I can communicate, that's why I can hear, smell and see! That's, why I feel psychic, I have intuition! My author gave all of these outstanding traits and qualities to me!

My creator was an author! An author gave me birth! Dare I say it, "my birth author"? Yes, my author loved me! I was born with love and tenderness. My author struggled with every word and phrase that it gave me. My author read me out loud and caressed me and smelled me. I was written, written on a "blank page" with a pen. Wow, another thought. My author might have written different books. Does that mean I have more relatives that I thought or that I could even imagine?

Then I realized that all of us had an author. We had all been born from love. We all had been loved! All of a sudden I felt an ocean of relief, RELIEF, wash over me. I hadn't even realized that I had been harboring so much anxiety within me. I didn't even care how old I was anymore, what is age anyway!

Oh, I have to tell B.P.! B.P. has so much to look forward too. Each word new and written! That means that B.P. will probably end up like me, in print. B.P. will be so disappointed. The important thing is not to forget that we all come from the same place, "A Blank Page."

I could tell that B.P. and that rest of the books on my shelf had thought I'd gone mad. By this time I was in a state of happiness. I needed to be alone and calm down and yet, I didn't want to be alone.

B.P. wasn't upset at all with all the new info I communicated. B.P. just took it as a matter of fact. It was refreshing to know that what I communicated had substance, and real meaning, at least as far as B.P was concerned and that B.P. trusted me.

I nestled myself next to B.P. I could feel that B.P. was very comfortable too. I could feel B.P. had something to communicate to me. "I knew what the meaning of author was after my first visit with Thesaurus." I wasn't even irritated. I just replied, "Why didn't you tell me?" B.P. responded, "You interrupted me and then you were being so weird, I thought I'd wait for the proper answer...

errr… I mean the right definition." Ohhhh" I replied and gently let my whole self drift off into space.

I started to get energy again. B.P., B.P., I kept it up until I got a response. I could feel that B.P. was aware of me. "You know what this means don't you?" B.P., sleepy reply was "What?" "What are you thinking now?"

This is what we have to do. We have a new goal or a new task. We need to let all the books know that they have been created, that they were born from an author, that they were created from love that we are all loved! This is our mission, but how are we going to accomplish this?"

B.P. s reply was, "I don't know, all I know is you can't be so pushy or obnoxious if you want a message like that to get out to the world of books." I thought about it and realized B.P. was right. I responded, "You are right, will you be by my side, will you help me, will you take this task on with me?" All I heard was a long drawn out, YYYEEEEESSSSSS.

Here's to New Beginning's
Yes to New Beginnings!